COOPER RIVER

CHARLESTON HARBOR

CONCORD STREET

WATERFRONT PARK

VENDUE

STATE STREET

EAST BAY STREET

CUMBERLAND STREET

CHURCH STREET

SOCIETY STREET

WENTWORTH STREET

HASEL STREET

MEETING STREET

MARKET STREET

KING STREET

ARCHDALE STREET

QUEEN STREET

BROAD STREET

TRADD STREET

MEETING STREET

KING STREET

EAST BATTERY

CHURCH STREET

SOUTH BATTERY

LEGARE STREET

MURRAY BLVD

BEAUFAIN STREET

RUTLEDGE AVENUE

COLONIAL LAKE

ASHLEY AVENUE

BROAD STREET

BLVD

U.S. COAST GUARD BASE

FORT SUMTER
NAVAL AND
MARITIME
MUSEUM

ASHLEY RIVER

HISTORIC
CHARLESTON,
SOUTH CAROLINA

ROSEBUD ROAMS
CHARLESTON

A CHILD'S CLIPPITY~CLOP GUIDE TO THE CITY
WRITTEN AND ILLUSTRATED BY SALLY SMITH

Legacy Publications

A Subsidiary of Pace Communications

Greensboro, North Carolina

I'd like to thank the many people—too many to list—who gave of themselves to advise, encourage,
show delight, brainstorm, support, read, keep their fingers crossed, listen, lift my hopes, get excited, give me reality checks,
edit, offer technical help, suggest, and, most of all, believe in me and the magic of Rosebud. You know who you are.
The list is long, and Rosebud would not be who she is without each and every one of you.

Story and Illustrations ©1999 / Sally Hughes Smith
Second Edition 2003

Design: Palmetto Graphic Design Company
ISBN 0-933101-19-8
Library of Congress Catalog Card Number 99-073720
Printed in Canada

For more information about Rosebud / www.sallysmith.com
Four prints from *Rosebud Roams Charleston* are available exclusively at the Gibbes Museum of Art, 135 Meeting Street,
Charleston, South Carolina 29401. 100% of the proceeds from the sales of these prints go to benefit the museum.

I dedicate this book to my family —

the one I grew up in,

the one I married into,

and the one C.D. and I built together —

and to people everywhere who work to build strong,

nurturing families of their own.

Now I was not always a city horse.

Oh, no.

I was born right under this giant oak tree

on an old plantation called Middleton Place.

A horse couldn't pick a finer place to grow up.

But I'm not like any horse you ever met.

I always dreamed of being somewhere else.

My mother named me Rosebud.

She thought I was prettier than any flower in the gardens that spring.

About the first thing I can remember is my daddy, a police horse

named Greenbud, telling me bedtime stories about a most unusual place

called Charleston, far away down the Ashley River.

Pretty soon all I wanted was to go there.

—

While the other horses ran and played, I would stand with

my nose turned toward Charleston, far away down the Ashley River.

My friends called me "silly," but I didn't mind.

"Let's buck and jump!" the colts and fillies called. "Let's leap and rear!"

"Not me," I'd say. "I just want to practice stopping at imaginary street corners

and nodding politely to strangers."

~

I liked pretending. I liked pretending to be a city horse.

Each night when Mother gave me a back tickle before bed,

I would tell her, "My dream is to go to Charleston!" She would nod her head and say,

"Rosebud, I hope your dream comes true, but I cannot see how you will ever

get to Charleston, far away down the Ashley River."

One day when I was almost grown up,

I saw an **AMAZING** thing: a great big truck full

of juicy orange carrots going down the road under the oaks.

Now carrots are like **CANDY** to me.

I licked my lips and took off after that delicious-looking truck.

I galloped down Ashley River Road, right past Drayton Hall and Magnolia Gardens.

Clippity-clop Clippity-clop after those carrots.

Finally the truck stopped, and I looked up.

When I saw where I was I forgot all about carrots. Right in front of me

was the tall steeple of St. Michael's Church! I was smack-dab in the middle

of Charleston, where I had dreamed of going all my life. Now was my chance

to see everything I had heard about in Daddy's stories.

I hurried over to White Point Gardens, where the Ashley and Cooper rivers

come together to form the great Atlantic Ocean. Strolling under the mossy oak trees,

I shivered when I read about the scary pirates who were captured there and

buried in the sand. And there was Fort Sumter, where Daddy said the

"War of the Late Unpleasantness" began. Children were climbing on the

heavy cannons and cannonballs left from the big battle.

Clippity-clop . . .

After going to see

the world's first submarine at the Charleston Museum,

~

I pranced past historic houses painted the colors of the rainbow on Rainbow Row.

How I grinned when I saw the "Hat Man," a funny picture

of a man made all out of people's hats painted on a wall on Church Street.

Clippity-clop . . .

It was a thrill to watch the dress parade at The Citadel.

Rows of marching soldiers carried dangerous-looking swords.

I thought I wanted to slide down that

amazing banister in The Nathaniel Russell House, until I saw how high it was!

Clippity-clop . . .

I especially liked visiting the damp and chilly
dungeon in the Old Exchange Building, but I didn't understand why
the tour guide fussed when I got hungry and started nibbling
some delicious hay from the exhibit!

In the evenings there was always something exciting
happening at the Dock Street Theatre, the oldest theater in America.

Clippity-clop . . .

Along the Battery,
I heard children laughing
up a storm. They were jumping
on a funny-looking thing
called a joggling board.
I laughed along with them.
"Will it hold me, too?" I asked.

By this time I had gotten quite good at all the city

things that I had practiced in the pasture, like stopping at street corners

and nodding politely to strangers.

It felt nice to hear people say, "What lovely manners she has," and,

"She may be 'from AWAY,' but she seems right at home in Charleston."

I began to receive some lovely invitations.

Clippity-clop . . .

I was asked to the peaceful courtyard of the

Confederate Home for tea and had a little taste of yummy she-crab soup.

Mr. Alston Rutledge Ravenel Rhett even invited me to a big Spoleto arts

festival party on his roof overlooking the harbor at sunset.

Clippity-clop . . .

Soon word reached the headmistress of the dancing school that

I was a good dancer, and she asked me to join her classes. I had to shop

up and down King Street before finally finding white gloves

big enough to fit me. What fun I was having!

One day I was enjoying looking at the beautiful paintings in the

Gibbes Museum of Art . . . until I saw a picture of Middleton Place. At once

I began to think of my dear mother and daddy, far away up the Ashley River.

I felt a little homesick, but only for a tiny second. After all,

hadn't I always wanted to live in Charleston?

I began to worry that someone
would come to take me back
to my pasture in the country.
I didn't want to think about that.
I was having too much fun
playing with the little children
each morning in
White Point Gardens, and . . .
Clippity-clop . . .

I certainly didn't want to miss my favorite treat, going to
Burbage's corner grocery every day at three. That's when nice Mr. Burbage always had a
crunchy carrot for me. Then it happened.

One day when I was making my rounds, a little boy pointed down the road
and said, "Look, Rosebud! Here comes a country horse!" Was someone coming to catch
me after all this time? I didn't even stop to see who it was. I began to run!

I put on my hat and tried to get lost in the crowds of tourists in the
City Market near those tasty-looking sweetgrass baskets.

Clippity-clop . . .

I got all wet hiding behind the pineapple fountain in Waterfront Park.

~

I ducked into a big dark open door to hide, and what do you think I saw?

Other horses! Other horses in big stalls, smiling at me!

A gray horse said, "Would you like to live here and pull carriages all over the city?"

"Yes!" I neighed.

*S*uddenly the horse running after me ran in the door, too,

and what a surprise! It was not someone trying to take me back,

but my own mother coming to see if I was all right.

"Rosebud," she said, "remember telling me your dream?

It has come true!"

~

I smiled a big smile. Mother began to smile, too.

We celebrated in a fancy restaurant with a yummy dinner of bean sprouts

and sugar cubes before she headed back to her home,

far away up the Ashley River.

That very evening I began happily

pulling carriages around the Charleston I love so much—and if I haven't

stopped pulling them, I'm pulling them still!

THE END ... almost

$\mathcal{W}$hy don't you visit my favorite places—

and lots of others I love too? I have listed some here and you will discover

others on your own. Have fun!

~

Listed below are points of particular historical interest located

on the map inside the front cover. Numbers are indicated in circles on the map.

The white circles indicate special children's programs.

1. CHARLESTON VISITOR CENTER, 375 Meeting Street across from Charleston Museum. Best place to start a visit.

2. BEST FRIEND MUSEUM, 31 Ann Street. See a full-size replica of the first train in regular passenger service in the U.S.

3. OLD CITADEL BUILDINGS, facing Marion Square. Built 1822, after attempted slave uprising, to house troops and arms; also housed military students. From this stemmed the South Carolina Military Academy.

4. SECOND PRESBYTERIAN CHURCH, 342–348 Meeting Street. Erected 1811.

5. MANIGAULT HOUSE, JOSEPH, 350 Meeting Street. Begun in 1802. Outstanding Adam architecture and view of Charleston life. Guided tours daily.

6. CHARLESTON MUSEUM, 360 Meeting Street. Oldest city museum in North America. Founded 1773. Replica of the first submarine, *The Hunley.*

7. ASHLEY HALL SCHOOL, 172 Rutledge Ave. Patrick Duncan House. Built about 1816.

8. THE CITADEL, founded in 1843. South Carolina Military College. Memorial Military Museum. Children enjoy seeing the dress parade at 3:45 p.m. every Friday during the school year.

9. ST. JOHANNES LUTHERAN CHURCH, corner Hasell and Anson. Built about 1810.

10. BETH ELOHIM SYNAGOGUE, 72 Hasell Street. Oldest U.S. synagogue in continuous use. Established 1750. Rebuilt 1838.

11. ST. MARY'S CHURCH, 89 Hasell Street. Mother church of the Roman Catholic Dioceses of the Carolinas and Georgia. Organized 1789. Present structure built 1838.

12. CONFEDERATE MUSEUM, 188 Meeting Street in Market Hall.

13. CITY MARKET, extending on Market Street from Meeting to East Bay. Established 1788. Houses shops, boutiques, flea market.

14. U.S. CUSTOM HOUSE, 200 East Bay. Started 1849. Stands on site of Craven Bastion. See marker.

15. OLD EXCHANGE BUILDING, East Bay, foot of Broad Street. One of the three most historically significant buildings of Colonial America. Built 1767–71 by the British on site of Court of Guard, where the pirate Stede Bonnet was imprisoned in 1718. An independent government was set up in this building by the Provincial Congress meeting in March 1776. George Washington was entertained here May 2, 1791. See Provost Dungeon where patriots were imprisoned.

16. DOCK STREET THEATRE, S.W. corner Church and Queen streets. Original theater opened 1736. Open to visitors.

17. FRENCH HUGUENOT CHURCH, S.E. corner of Church and Queen streets. Site of three successive Huguenot churches. Present edifice begun 1844. Only Huguenot church in America adhering exactly to the liturgy of the French Protestant Church.

18. WATERFRONT PARK, Relax and enjoy harbor breezes. Children love the fountain. See markers on city history.

19. THOMAS ELFE WORKSHOP, 54 Queen Street. Built prior to 1760. Perfectly scaled miniature of a single house. Open to visitors.

20. ST. PHILIP'S PROTESTANT EPISCOPAL CHURCH, Church Street north of Queen. First building, circa 1690. Present building begun 1835. In its two cemeteries lie many distinguished South Carolinians. Grave of John C. Calhoun.

21. OLD POWDER MAGAZINE, 23 Cumberland. Constructed 1711. Used during the Revolutionary War as a powder storehouse. Open to visitors.

22. 134 MEETING STREET, site of Institute Hall, where the Ordinance of Secession was signed on December 20, 1860. See marker.

23. CIRCULAR CONGREGATIONAL CHURCH, 138–150 Meeting Street. Organized 1681. First church known as White Meeting House, giving Meeting Street its name. Church of circular form begun in 1804. Present structure 1891.

24. GIBBES MUSEUM OF ART, 135 Meeting Street. Houses many valuable paintings and special exhibits. Fine portrait and miniature collection. Japanese prints, small-scale reproduction rooms. Classes. Lectures. Shop (the only shop in Charleston offering Rosebud prints for sale to benefit the museum).

25. HIBERNIAN HALL, 105 Meeting Street. Home of Hibernian Society, founded March 17, 1801. See marker.

26. FIREPROOF BUILDING, Meeting Street at Chalmers. First fireproof building erected in the U.S. Begun in 1822. Robert Mills, architect. See marker.

27. CITY HALL, N.E. corner of Meeting and Broad streets. Erected 1801 as a bank office. Purchased by the City in 1818. Council Chamber houses portraits of important leaders, including Trumbull's famous portrait of General Washington. See marker.

28. COUNTY COURT HOUSE, N.W. corner of Meeting and Broad streets. Begun as State House 1752. Burned 1788 and rebuilt on old walls. Court House since 1790. See marker.

29. U.S. POST OFFICE AND FEDERAL COURT, S.W. corner of Broad and Meeting streets. Site of City Guard House destroyed in earthquake, 1886. Postal museum.

30. ST. MICHAEL'S PROTESTANT EPISCOPAL CHURCH, S.E. corner of Broad and Meeting streets. Established 1751. Its bells have crossed the Atlantic Ocean five times. George Washington and the Marquis de Lafayette worshipped here when visiting Charleston. Two signers of the Declaration of Independence are buried here.

31. SOUTH CAROLINA SOCIETY HALL, 72 Meeting Street. Designed by Gabriel Manigault; built 1804.

32. HEYWARD~WASHINGTON HOUSE, 87 Church Street. Begun about 1770. Home of Thomas Heyward, signer of the Declaration of Independence. George Washington was entertained here in May 1791. Open to visitors.

33. VANDERHORST ROW, 78 East Bay. 1800. Three dwellings in one structure. One of the first such buildings in America.

34. FIRST BAPTIST CHURCH, 61–65 Church Street. Oldest Baptist congregation in S.C. Present church begun 1819.

35. EDMONSTON~ALSTON HOUSE, 21 East Battery. Built in 1828, redecorated in the ornate Greek Revival style in 1838, contains original family furniture and decorative arts. General Beauregard watched the bombardment of Fort Sumter from its piazza. Open to visitors.

36. CALHOUN MANSION, 16 Meeting Street. Elegant Victorian mansion with 24,000 square feet of rooms and ornate interior. Built circa 1876. Open to visitors.

37. NATHANIEL RUSSELL HOUSE, 51 Meeting Street. Built in 1808, renowned for its flying stairs, spiraling unsupported for three floors, and important period furnishings. Guided tours daily.

38. FIRST (SCOTS) PRESBYTERIAN CHURCH, S.W. corner of Meeting and Tradd streets. Organized 1731. See marker.

39. CATHEDRAL OF ST. JOHN THE BAPTIST, N.E. corner of Broad and Legare streets. Original cathedral dedicated 1821, burned 1861. Present structure 1907. Stars on its bricks were stamped by hand.

40. CHARLESTON LIBRARY SOCIETY, 164 King Street. Organized 1748.

41. UNITARIAN CHURCH, 4 Archdale Street. Begun 1772, completed 1787; remodeled 1852. Interesting interior.

42. ST. JOHN'S LUTHERAN CHURCH,
10–12 Archdale Street. First church 1759. Present building (third) 1818.

43. GRACE PROTESTANT EPISCOPAL CHURCH,
Wentworth near Glebe Street. Established 1847. Lovely interior.

44. COLLEGE OF CHARLESTON,
George and Philip streets. Founded in 1770. Oldest municipal college in America.

45. BETHEL M.E. CHURCH, S.W. corner Calhoun and Pitt streets. Earlier church built 1797–1809. Present structure 1853.

46. CHARLESTON METRO CHAMBER OF COMMERCE,
America's oldest local chamber of commerce, located at 81 Mary Street in Gas Engine Building originally used by the S.C. Railroad.

47. HISTORIC CHARLESTON FOUNDATION,
40 East Bay. Dedicated to preserving the historic fabric of Charleston.

48. HAMPTON PARK, spacious park beside The Citadel. Biking trails, duck pond, former site of famous Charleston racetrack.

49. RAINBOW ROW, south of Broad on East Bay Street. Colorful row of houses that originally served as stores and dwellings.

50. WHITE POINT GARDENS, lovely public park at the tip of the peninsula. A Civil War battery with old cannons. See markers on High Battery walk.

51. HAT MAN MURAL, S.E. corner of Church and Broad streets. Site of old haberdashery.

52. THE CHARLESTON PRESERVATION SOCIETY,
147 King Street. The nation's oldest community-based preservation organization.

53. CONFEDERATE HOME AND COLLEGE,
62 Broad Street. Home and college for Civil War widows and orphans. See marker.

54. AIKEN~RHETT HOUSE, 48 Elizabeth Street. National Historic Register. Palatial antebellum mansion with outbuildings. Open to visitors.

55. BURBAGE'S, 157 Broad Street. Old-style neighborhood grocery. (Rosebud's favorite!)

56. OLD ST. ANDREW'S PARISH CHURCH, Picturesque, historic church on Hwy. 61 on way to plantations.

57. CHARLES TOWNE LANDING, Hwy 171. One of the sites of the original settlement of Charleston in April 1670. 80 acres of landscaped gardens. The Animal Forest features animals indigenous to S.C. A full-scale replica of a 17th-century trading vessel is moored in Olde Towne Creek. Bike trails.

58. MAGNOLIA GARDENS, 10 mi. N.W. on Hwy. 61. America's oldest garden (circa 1680). Boasts one of the largest collections of azaleas and camellias in the country. Audubon Swamp Garden, plantation house, and petting zoo.

59. DRAYTON HALL, 9 mi. N.W. on Hwy. 61. Built circa 1738, survived the Civil War intact. The house is preserved in almost original condition. One of the finest examples of Georgian Palladian architecture in the nation. National Historic Landmark.

60. MIDDLETON PLACE, 11 mi. N.W. on Hwy. 61. America's oldest landscaped garden, including butterfly lakes (1741). Also Plantation Stableyards and Middleton Place House. National Historic Landmark. Rosebud's home.

61. PATRIOT'S POINT, Charleston Harbor in Mount Pleasant. Home of the famous World War II aircraft carrier *Yorktown*, also submarine, destroyer, Coast Guard cutter, Medal of Honor Museum, and 25 vintage aircraft.

62. FORT SUMTER NAVAL AND MARITIME MUSEUM, may be visited by private boat or tour boat. Man-made island in Charleston Harbor. On April 12, 1861, Confederate forces at Fort Johnson fired the first shot of the Civil War at the Union-occupied Fort Sumter.

63. SOUTH CAROLINA AQUARIUM, 3250 Concord Street. More than 60 exhibits display and interpret state's diverse habitat, with, 10,000 organisms, representing 500 species. Very popular with children, especially on rainy days.

64. CHILDREN'S MUSEUM OF THE LOWCOUNTRY, Opening fall 2003—look for it!

65. MUSEUM ON THE COMMON, 217 Lucas Street, Mt. Pleasant. A multi-sensory exhibit places you in the aftermath of Hurricane Hugo.

66. SHEM CREEK MARITIME MUSEUM, 514 Mill Street, Mt. Pleasant. Chronicles the story of the Charleston area's rich maritime heritage. Working boat-builder on site.

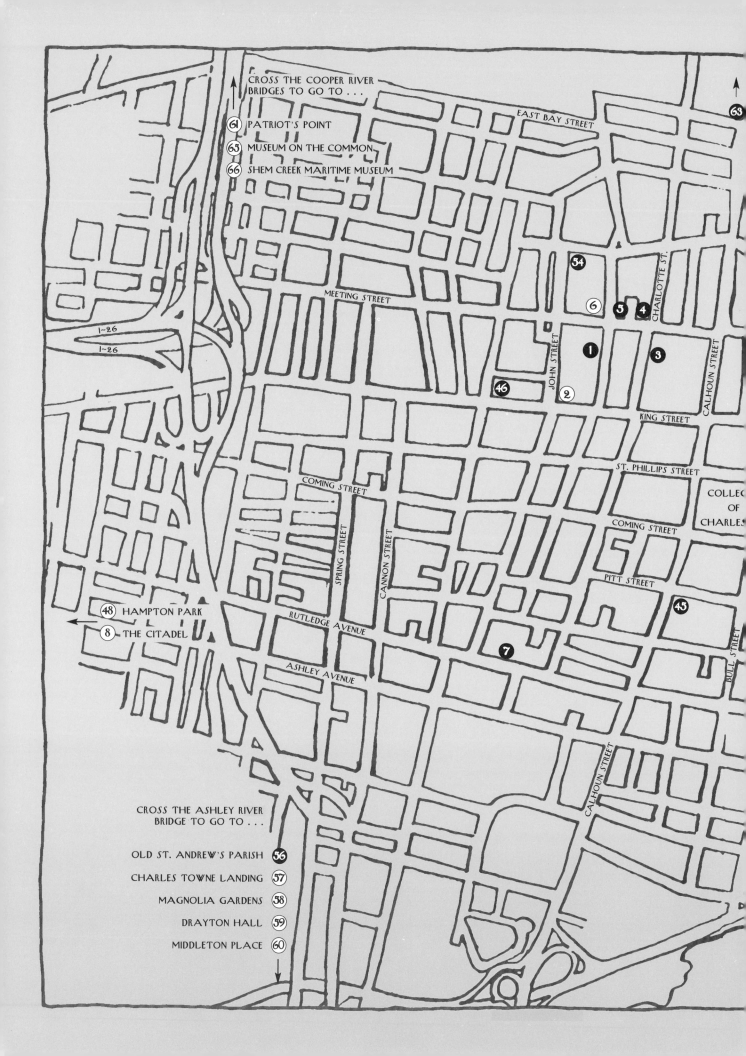

CROSS THE COOPER RIVER
BRIDGES TO GO TO . . .

(61) PATRIOT'S POINT

(65) MUSEUM ON THE COMMON

(66) SHEM CREEK MARITIME MUSEUM

EAST BAY STREET

(63)

(54)

MEETING STREET

(6) (5) (4)

CHARLOTTE ST.

(1) (3)

JOHN STREET

CALHOUN STREET

(46) (2)

KING STREET

ST. PHILLIPS STREET

COMING STREET

COLLEGE
OF
CHARLES.

COMING STREET

SPRING STREET

CANNON STREET

PITT STREET

(45)

(48) HAMPTON PARK

RUTLEDGE AVENUE

(8) THE CITADEL

(7)

BULL STREET

ASHLEY AVENUE

CALHOUN STREET

CROSS THE ASHLEY RIVER
BRIDGE TO GO TO . . .

OLD ST. ANDREW'S PARISH (56)

CHARLES TOWNE LANDING (57)

MAGNOLIA GARDENS (58)

DRAYTON HALL (59)

MIDDLETON PLACE (60)

I-26

I-26